A Hero Is

Written & illustrated by Nikki Rogers

A hero is not afraid to stand
against those who are violent.
He knows that evil men will rule
if good men just keep silent.

A hero like a fireman
is strong and very brave.
He'll risk his life if there is
someone else that he can save.

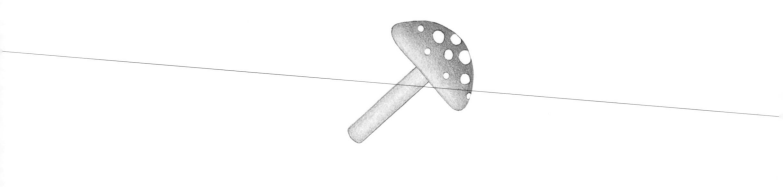

A hero cares for nature
and every living thing.
And as he works to help the earth
he hears creation sing.

A hero is a loyal friend.
He's honorable and brave.
He fights for truth and
does what's right
even if he's afraid.

A hero is alert and ready.
He knows just what to do.
If someone is in danger
he will race to their rescue.

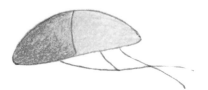

A hero uses what he has
to help all those in need.
He thinks of others
before himself
not driven by power or greed.

A hero fixes broken things.
He likes to make things better.
Using the talents that he has
he's helpful and he's clever.

A hero works hard at his job
and always does his best,
not just to meet his own needs
but so others can be blessed.

A hero creates solutions
to problems that we face.
He invents and thinks of ways
to make the world
a better place.

A hero is a dad who loves
his wife and family.
He teaches and empowers them
to be all they can be.

A hero is compassionate,
honest in word and deed,
faithful, strong, courageous
and sets the people free.
Every boy can be a hero,
brave knight or superman
by helping others, doing right
and being the best he can!

🐦 About the Author

I am a mother of two, a girl and a boy.
I originally started writing children's
stories with values that I wanted to instil
in my own children, and I hope to share these messages
with children all over the world.

All my children's books are written with the desire to
inspire both children and adults to be all they were
created to be.

Any profit from these books is used to support various
world missions that help causes close to my heart.

For more information about
the inspiration behind this book

Written with love for my son, Josiah,
and every little hero in the world.

For more info, lesson plans & FREE resources
visit www.createdtobe.com.au
eBooks also available
Like us at www.facebook.com/created.to.be.you

☻ **www.createdtobe.com.au**

Inspirational Children's Books by Nikki Rogers

A Beautiful Girl is a lovely book that celebrates the beautiful diversity in every girl. With beautiful illustrations accompanied by poetry, little girls and big girls will love this book that inspires them to shine the beauty within.

A Hero Is explores the characteristics of what makes a hero and just how diverse heroes can be. With vibrant illustrations accompanied by poetry this book will inspire little boys to be heroes in their everyday life.

The Garden In My Heart is a thoughtful book about sowing and reaping that encourages children to sow good things in their heart. We all have a garden that can produce flowers of joy or weeds of jealousy and bitterness.

Rainbow Moments is a colorful book that explores some of the ways God can speak to us. It encourages the reader to stop, look, listen and recognize the special moments when God reminds us of His love and promises.

What Love Looks Like is a delightful book that looks at the many different ways people give and receive love and can help you identify what makes you and others feel loved the most. Inspired by *The 5 Love Languages*®.

Sooty & Snow is a book about boundaries. It is a fun and colorful book about an adventurous chicken who insists on finding ways to get over the fence. Will Sooty realize that the fence is there because she is loved?

Wilbur the Woolly is a book about trusting the good shepherd. Follow Wilbur the sheep on his journey as he learns to trust in the shepherd's love for him and discovers that getting his own way isn't always best.

52055317R00018

Made in the USA
Lexington, KY
14 May 2016